WATER SAFETY WITH SWIMMY

10 Water Safety Rules Everyone Should Follow

Carolanne Caron

Illustrated by Rebecca Laidlaw

LifeRich Publishing is a registered trademark of The Reader's Digest Association, Inc.

LifeRich Publishing books may be ordered through booksellers or by contacting:

LifeRich Publishing
1663 Liberty Drive
Bloomington, IN 47403
www.liferichpublishing.com
1 (888) 238-8637

Because of the dynamic nature of the Internet, any web addresses or links contained in this book may have changed since publication and may no longer be valid. The views expressed in this work are solely those of the author and do not necessarily reflect the views of the publisher, and the publisher hereby disclaims any responsibility for them.

ISBN: 978-1-4897-0747-5 (sc)
ISBN: 978-1-4897-0750-5 (e)

Library of Congress Control Number: 2016960654

Print information available on the last page.

LifeRich Publishing rev. date: 04/13/2018

Disclaimer:

At Winning Swimming, we are very serious about doing our part to decrease the potential for drowning and are introducing this book as a supplement for existing Water Safety or swimming programs. This book should not be used as a substitute for qualified swim lessons or water safety instruction.

If you would like more information about our Learn to Swim program, other Water Safety Resources in this series, or have any questions please visit our websites at www.WinningSwimming.com or www.WaterSafetywithSwimmy.com.

Happy Swimming,
Carolanne Caron, Head Coach
Winning Swimming L.L.C.

"Hi! My name is Swimmy and I'm so excited you've come to learn about water safety.

First, let's meet my friends."

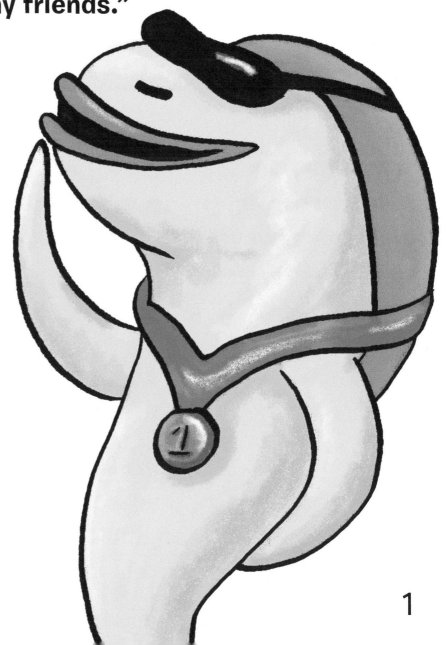

"Hi, I'm Sydney the Seahorse. I'm little and cannot swim so I always have an adult swimming right next to me."

"I'm Sandy the Starfish and I'm starting to learn to swim so I stay in the shallow end and always have an adult next to me."

"I'm Finley the Fish. I know how to float and get to the side so I have an adult in the water with me and within arm's reach."

"I'm Flip the Frog and I know how to do Freestyle and Backstroke so I can go in the deep end and just need an adult watching me."

"Hi, I'm Danny the Dolphin. I know all the strokes and am training for the swim team."

"Now that you know everyone, are you ready to learn about Water Safety?

Great! Let's go..."

4

Water Safety is so fun
In the pool, or lake, or tub.
On a nice and sunny day,
Sunscreen on right away.
This is the first of our rules.
Now it's time for the pool.

At the pool and no-one's here.
Should we swim? The water's clear.
Before you go near any water
Look for the lifeguard or a spotter.
An adult needs to watch you, too.
This is rule number two.

Before we swim in the pool,
Read the sign with all the rules:
Use walking feet on the deck.

Don't push or shove or you will sit.
Never potty in the pool.
This is the third of all the rules.

When you are on a boat,
Wear a life jacket that floats.
If you cannot swim too well,
Wear it in the pool as well.
Rule number four will be
The best one for you and me.

When you want to go and swim,
Always have someone you're with.
A buddy is what you need.
Two is safer than one indeed.
Remember a buddy at your side
Is the key to rule number five.

Now we are ready to swim.
Look before you leap and then
Always first with your feet

Unless the water is plenty deep.
Look first and go with your feet.
Rule number six, it can't be beat.

Next, if you cannot swim,
Stay where you can touch and then
Don't panic if your face gets wet.

16

Use bubbles and you're all set.
Staying shallow is best for you.
Guess what, we are almost through.

"Help, help" you hear them shout.
How can you get them out?
Reach or throw but never go.

Use a long stick while you're low.
A tube or ring that floats to throw.
Your blow up toy won't help them though.

If it's stormy, lightning, or thunder,
Get out quick and take cover.
Go inside away from water.
Listen to lifeguards and the spotters.
Wait 30 minutes before going back
From the last thunder clap.

20

Finally, learn to swim and float.
Having fun is what we hope.
Blowing bubbles, kicking feet

Being safe with all we meet.
Now it's time to get out.
Please don't cry, fuss, or pout.

**Water Safety is so fun
In the pool or lake or tub.
Remember the rules are for you,
Your buddy, parents, and your crew.
We hope that you've had some fun.
Water safety is number ONE!**

25

1. Wear sunscreen.

2. Swim only when a lifeguard or an adult is watching.

3. Follow the rules on the signs and the lifeguard's instructions.

4. Wear a life jacket if you cannot swim and always on a boat.

5. Swim with a buddy.

Water Safety

6. Look before you leap and go in feet first.

7. Stay where you can touch and use your bubbles if your face goes under.

8. To assist someone in trouble, reach with a pole or throw a float.

9. Take cover if you see a storm, see lightning, or hear thunder.

10. Learn to swim and float!

Rule Review

For more information about our Learn to Swim program,
other Water Safety Resources in this series,
or if you have any questions, please visit our websites at
www.WinningSwimming.com or
www.WaterSafetywithSwimmy.com

About the Author:

Carolanne Caron a/k/a "Coach Caron" has been swimming her whole life. Starting swim lessons at age 1 was a necessity because her mother did not know how to swim. Her mom insisted the children learn to swim because if anything happened around the water, mom would not be able to save them.

Swimming lessons was the best gift Coach Caron's mother could have given her. Growing up with a love of the water lead to working at the town pool as a lifeguard and a swim instructor, swimming on the high school women's team, and managing the high school men's team. After having children of her own, Coach Caron decided there was a need to teach children and adults in her area to swim so she opened Winning Swimming, LLC.

Next came the idea to teach local preschool children how to be safer in the water. When Coach Caron had a hard time finding an appropriate book about water safety to read to the children, she wrote Water Safety with Swimmy.

Coach Caron teaches at Winning Swimming LLC in Merrimack, New Hampshire, USA and holds certifications from The American Red Cross, USA Swimming, American Swim Coaches Association, Precision Nutrition, and is an approved water safety presenter in the State of New Hampshire.

For more information, please visit
www.WinningSwimming.com or
www.WaterSafetywithSwimmy.com